# AFTER THIS

# AFTER THIS

---

## LIFE, DEATH & THE JUDGMENT

---

Randall Johnson

RANDALL JOHNSON Publisher

# Contents


*Dedication*                                        vii

Preface                                               3

  1  THE OBSERVER                   6

  2  MEET FRANK                      9

  3  MEET SOPHIE                    12

  4  MEET CASSIE                    15

  5  MEET STEPHEN                   17

  6  MEET DAVID                     20

  7  MEET JAMIE                     23

  8  FRANK'S BACKGROUND             26

  9  SOPHIE'S BACKGROUND            29

10  CASSIE'S BACKGROUND             32

11  STEPHEN'S BACKGROUND            34

12  DAVID'S BACKGROUND              37

13  JAMIE'S BACKGROUND              40

14  FRANK'S ENCOUNTER              42

**15**  SOPHIE'S LEGACY  46

**16**  CASSIE'S DOWNFALL  49

**17**  STEPHEN'S SCHEDULE  52

**18**  DAVID'S ROOMATE  54

**19**  JAMIE'S DIAGNOSIS  57

**20**  THE OBSERVER'S PLEA  62

**21**  FRANK'S DEMISE  64

**22**  SOPHIE'S REST  67

**23**  CASSIE'S CHOICE  69

**24**  STEPHEN'S FINAL FLIGHT  71

**25**  DAVID'S LAST EMBRACE  73

**26**  JAMIE'S PRAYER  75

**27**  THE SIX BRETHREN  77

**28**  THE OBSERVER REVEALED  80

**29**  STEPHEN WRIGHT!  83

**30**  CASSANDRA DANIELS!  86

**31**  FRANK BENJAMIN! SOPHIIE CAMPBELL! DAVID CARPENTER! JAMIE RAMSEY!  89

Epilogue: The Observer  93

About The Author  94

This book is dedicated
to my wife,

CINDY

ISBN: 979-8-9859130- 3-3 (SC)

ISBN: 979-8-9859130-4-0 (E)

BISAC FIC027000; REL030000; REL067060

Second Printing, 2022

Published by RS Johnson Publishers in Rochester, NY

Cover design by Randall Johnson

Epigraph


"And it is appointed unto men once to die, but ***after this*** the judgment."
Hebrews 9:27 KJV

# Preface

Having retired from over thirty years in a corporate career, my expectations of a future was to settle into retirement and then perhaps see if something develops. My faith dictates I must move when prompted by God so, as humbly as I can, I offer this volume as a response to the urging of the Holy Spirit.

This work began as a vague calling to write a book. An unusual calling in that my least favorite class in school was English. I wasn't sure what the subject would be, but over several weeks the premise and subject of this work, was slowly revealed to me. I bounced the concept off my wife, whose wisdom in these matters I cherish, and she confirmed that I should proceed. Proceed to what end I was not sure. Only God can prosper this work going forth, so I am doing my part and leaving the rest to God.

This work is a creation of pure fiction. All of the characters herein are figments of my imagination, none are real nor are they based on real people. However, they do reflect human characteristics, thoughts, emotions, failures, successes, limitations, frailties and feelings. It has been my intent that any similarities of the characters in this novel, to any living person is purely coincidental. I offer my profound apologies to anyone who may seem to be portrayed herein, and please realize that the situations are strictly fictitious, although fairly typical of what can occur in real life.

Further, I have striven to depict situations in life and how the Word of God addresses those situations with blessings and consequences. The verse "... A man reaps what he sows." (GAL 6:8) applies specifically in this work. The depiction of all events pre- and post-death are, as I envision, based on my study of scripture. Anything that approaches the reality of post-life circumstances came to me as a result of the revelation of the Holy Spirit. Anything that deviates from that reality can only be a result of the limited knowledge and interpretation of this humble servant.

It is my wish that the reader ponders this work, perhaps a comparison to a character or two may be relevant, but please look beyond what is written herein, and seek to apply the underlying concepts to the particulars of your individual life. I do not have the answers to the great mysteries of life, but I do know some guiding principles, and I know the Savior to whom I can count on, that I hope, has been portrayed herein.

Foremost, I wish to acknowledge the encouragement and insight given to this book by my lovely wife and best friend, Cindy, in heartfelt gratitude for being my life-partner. Thank you for your support to bring this work to fruition along with your proofreading and editing contributions.

# BEFORE THIS

# 1

## THE OBSERVER

Welcome! As you look around you may have noticed this room, this table and chair and overhead lighting is about as generic as you can imagine. There are no memorable colors, no lingering odors, no noticeable change in temperature, nor any background noise to distract. You may wonder how you got here since there is no 'here' here. As you can see, there is nothing about our surroundings that in any form or fashion will give you a clue as to where you are: you are just here. You got here by opening a book and letting your mind take you away from there. So now you are here, and you are with me.

You will be accompanying me on this morning of August 23$^{rd}$. Now that may not be the time or date on your calendar before you came here, but that is where we are. Your presence with me is extremely rare. In fact, I am not exactly sure how you were approved to take this tour considering your present 'alive' condition. However, I am not to question why, but just to do my job. There are three guiding principles you must follow if you wish to remain on with me and a failure to obey them will result in expulsion or might even justify an early termination.

- Please do not ask questions. If you do not understand any-thing, please be assured that you eventually will.
- Please do not offer your opinions or suggestions as to how I should do my job. Rest assured that I do my job very well and have been doing it a lot longer than you have been around.
- Lastly, and most importantly, do not interfere in any way, shape or form. This is strictly prohibited.

You are here for one reason, and one reason only, and that is to witness 'the process.' You may only use your eyes and ears in your witnessing. You cannot take any notes, pictures or recordings. You can only take away from this tour what you remember. Nothing else. If you have any questions you may ask them now, otherwise, from here forward, silence is an absolute requirement.

My name is not important now, but rest assured my identity will eventually be revealed. If you must have a name to remember me by, just use the name "Observer" since that describes some of what I do although certainly not the entirety of all that I am.

I want you to pay particular attention to the fact that, on this tour, we will become invisible to those around us. You will not know how we are able to do this, but please realize that anonymity is critical to the work that I perform.

Additionally, when I speak, you and you alone will be able to hear me unless I am also speaking to someone else in which case both of you can hear me but no one else. We also will have the ability to hear people's thoughts. This is a vital method we rely upon in evaluating motives, intent, emotions, and desires.

You will become aware that, on this tour, time has a way of fold-ing on itself allowing us to appear in multiple, distant places at the same time. So that you do not become too confused as to time and place, I will separate locations and allow you to visit each person sequentially at the same moment.

Although I mostly observe, there will be occasions when I actively do my best to persuade, prod, cajole, nudge, implore and convince people to take specific actions. These actions are all directed toward the benefit of our fellow brethren. Some of them have trained their ear to listen to me and respond, while others do not have any clue.

You will follow me today as I observe six individuals: Frank, Sophie, Stephen, Cassie, David and Jamie. There is more to be revealed, but that's as much as I will tell you for now. Please observe.

# 2

# MEET FRANK

8:30 AM. In a split second, you may have observed, we are now in a bedroom right next to a bed. This is Frank, Frank Benjamin. Age thirty-two. Married to Darla, also thirty-two, and they have two kids: Adam seven and Katie three. They live in Marion, Indiana and, well, that's enough background for now, let's observe Frank:

...

The alarm clock wailed on Frank's nightstand pulling his conscience back to reality from the dopey dream he was having. With a well-trained wave of his arm, he exactly smacked the snooze button and silence re-entered the room. Moments later Frank struggled out of bed, his aching joints pleading for more rest. After negotiating the toilet, he was soon in the hot shower with shampoo stinging his eyes. His mind drifted to recall his strange dream, but details escaped his still fuzzy brain. After he dragged a comb through his hair and a quick shave, he plodded back to the bedroom and dressed in his work clothes as he had done countless times. Frank was a big man tipping the scales at 280 and was built to work in the construction trade. Strong arms, calloused hands, steady back and quick on his feet, he took the long hours on work sites in stride always having enough left in the tank for his home life. A final splash of Darla's favorite cologne and he headed downstairs to the brewing coffee and his two boisterous kids.

"Daddy, Adam is teasing my dolls again!" complained his stunningly beautiful three-year old daughter.

Adam continued with his cereal at the breakfast table with that impish grin on his face, having been caught provoking his sister. "She started it first!" he threw in just to placate his dad. "Hi pops!"

"Just stop it." Was all that Frank could muster this early in the morning. "Be nice to your sister." "Hi honey, how's my sweetheart today?" he cooed to his beautiful bride Darla, while lifting her off her feet with a twirl and a bear hug.

"Frank! The kids!" she half protested while knowingly wanting more. "Sit down and eat your breakfast, it will be cold soon. Remember, you have a big day at work today!"

"Don't I know it! Those last five houses have to be done by next week or else Hudson Construction will have to pay late penalties. If we finish on time, we both know who will get a big fat bonus! Ooooweee!" Frank gave a fist pump while gobbling down his breakfast and juice. He grabbed his lunch box and travel mug of hot coffee and, standing up, announced "Got to go now! Bye kids!" Frank bent down and kissed Katie on the cheek. She giggled and gave her daddy a big hug. He then high fived Adam and lifted him up to the ceiling while spinning around. Adam always anticipated this ritual and feigned disapproval but loved it every time.

Frank headed for the door but couldn't resist one more squeeze as he picked her up, hugged her and kissed her: the love of his life, his one, his only, Darla. "Bye darling. I love you with all my heart!" he said as he slowly let her down.

"Me too Frank! Be careful today." Darla reassured as she did every morning.

The squeaky hinges on the back screen door groaned as the door opened and then slammed behind him. Darla and the kids watched him until he climbed into his pickup and the engine started with a roar. Gravel crunched under the tires as he pulled out the driveway and headed down the dusty road.

# 3

---

# MEET SOPHIE

8:30 AM. We will leave Frank for a moment, and you will now meet Sophie Campbell. Sophie is a widow of over seventy-years and recently celebrated her 102<sup>nd</sup> birthday. She lives in a comfortable nursing home in Biloxi, Mississippi and had four kids who are now all senior citizens. Let's observe:

...

Sophie sat in the dining hall at the Biloxi Senior Center and Nursing Home picking through her scrambled eggs and cold toast. She had lost her appetite for such breakfasts a number of years ago when things just didn't seem to sit well in her stomach. Funny thing is that's just about all that has ever gone south as far as her health was concerned. She has been fit as a fiddle her whole life and the doctors and nurses at the home were amazed that she did not need any meds, especially at her age! Sophie also had a mind like a steel trap and could remember in vivid detail events from her distant past as though they occurred just yesterday.

"More coffee mam?" the aide pleasantly asked.

"No, thankya. I believe I've had enough this mornin'." Sophie offered with a wry smile and a twinkle in her eye. "The kids are supposed to be comin' for lunch today and I have to save up my appetite for them." She reflected a moment then added "I do want to thank you Suzy for all you have done for me over the last few years. I know us old folks are a bit cranky at times, but you have taken it all in with such grace. I surely hope the Lord blesses you and your family." Again, that twinkle brightened in Sophie's eyes as she knew Suzy would blush at the compliment and the good wishes. Sophie delighted in passing out her gratitude and compliments always saying, "a good smile always brightens a day."

Sophie slowly rose to her feet, her well-worn walker with the bike horn and the plastic daisy flowers suited her slow but steady gait. Her ninety-five-pound soaking wet frame barely filled out a size two dress and the clomping of her tight laced leather shoes could be heard echoing through the halls of the home. Stomp, stomp, clunk. She inched along with her walker. Stomp, stomp, clunk.

Sophie could just as easily be mistaken as a "Daisy" due to her fondness for daisies. Her tiny room was fully decorated with all things 'daisy'. She loved the "He loves me, he loves me not" rhyme from her childhood days and always found a way to end on "He loves me!" with a great big satisfying grin. It was never certain who it was that caught her eye and her desire to be loved. You could guess it was her long-deceased husband, but she would never tell. She would always flash that smile with her twinkle and remain silent. Everyone knew that meant to not ask any more questions.

The staff at the home knew this would be a big day for Sophie. Her great-great-granddaughter was getting married in town today and before all the festivities the whole wedding party, which also meant her whole extended family, was stopping by to see her before the big event. Sophie just didn't have the stamina anymore for such festivities so instead of bringing her to the wedding they would bring some of the wedding to her. The staff had earlier laid out the new 'daisy' dress her son had purchased for her and she was so looking forward to absorbing all the love that the family was going to bestow upon her today. Her twinkle seemed to sparkle ever so brighter.

# 4

# MEET CASSIE

5:30AM – west coast time: Next I want you to meet Cassandra Daniels who goes by Cassie. Age is fifty-eight. Never married but has a partner – Rhonda of thirty-seven years. Both hail from Texas, but currently live in Sacramento.

...

The earliest glow of morning light, signaling the end of another hopeless night, slowly made its way into Cassie's bedroom. The dawning of the new day brought with it hope of an end to the torment Cassie had endured through the night. Pain and suffering through the fog of cancer, morphine and Quaaludes left Cassie in a drug induced stupor that she loathed to emerge from. The days were turning into nights and into days with regularity these past few weeks as Cassie sunk deeper and deep into the canyon of dying. Her youthful and middle age beauty were long faded and consumed by her disease leaving behind a skeletonized look more befitting a corpse than the living. Her pallor was ashen, her breathing shallow, her attitude, when offered, worse than surly. She was lonely but not alone. She wanted solitude but was denied due to the past romance and long obligation of her dedicated lover Rhonda.

The storm that only moments ago was on the horizon, occasionally flashing burst of light was now upon the Daniel's home with torrents of rain pounding against the steel roof of their two-story condo. Lightning flashes lit up the bedroom and then plunged it back into gloom. The immediate crack of loud thunder signaled the lightning was upon them and the room shook under the ferocity of the weather. One would have to look far and wide to find a more somber room for the dying. Grief hung in the air like a bad cigar and the palpable misery within Cassie only further depressed the promise of the new day.

Rhonda, if nothing else was true to the end. She had been with Cassie through thick and thin over the past three decades and though the end was near she could not abandon Cassie even though her heart now belonged somewhere else. Rhonda had found a new love and was anxious to re-ignite her life as soon as she could. The passing hours had really strained her dedication to Cassie. The inevitable was as certain as the Stage IV pancreatic cancer was working its last evil within Cassie's withering bowels. Rhonda wanted their relationship to be over and Cassie wanted her life to end.

Both were just waiting. The disease was taking its time and the time was crawling so slowly. There were no more medicines for relief, no more hope of a better day, no more joy in shared time together, only the anticipated and expected end.

They were waiting, and waiting was torture.

# 5

# MEET STEPHEN

8:30 AM: Next you will see quite a different situation while observing Stephen Boyd Wright, a forty-year-old Multimillionaire who was born into wealth and multiplied it. Now living in New York, let's visit and observe Stephen:

...

The gentle rain had been falling on the window of his ninth-floor corner office all morning. Dreary would have been a good word to describe the weather and his melancholy mood. Stephen Boyd Wright the third had reached the apex of Academia and he was idolized in the social circles he traveled. His renown in the Environmental Sciences was never questioned and the framed diplomas and honoraria fully covered two walls of his substantial office. Money was something that just didn't concern him anymore as his riches multiplied yearly from the many books he had authored and speeches he had given. He had made it and made it big and he was bored, perhaps even depressed.

Steve dressed for success. His Armani suits were expertly tailored to fit the physique chiseled through hours in the gym. His stature at

5' 5" was his one regret. He always wanted to be taller and often put wedges in his shoes to squeeze out another half-inch. Maybe this is what drove him so much to excel with a "Success is better than stature" tape constantly playing in his mind.

His personal and professional staffs saw to his every need. Rarely did he have to request anything that he wanted. Stephen paid them well to anticipate his needs and he was rarely disappointed. Food, entertainment, transportation was always available. He had everything he wanted except his life was empty. He felt no challenge in life anymore, he felt controlled by the ambitious travel schedule intended to feed the fires of the financial monster he created and directed. The next five months of his life are defined and booked with no room for changes or cancellations. Stephen constantly avoided contact with people as a cold or flu germ could derail his finely tuned schedule. Getting sick was just not an option and his staff strived to guarantee it.

Stephen spent the early morning finishing his daily updates on the financial markets, weather conditions for key US cities and reviewing his packed agenda. He rehearsed the opening thoughts he would share for each of his stops throughout the day and made sure the staff had packed all the necessary papers in the briefcase.

"Excuse me Mr. Boyd. I have a Mr. Bennett on hold from Houston. He is requesting a firm ETA for the airport limo. I know you are quite close to him and thought I should check with you before giving him the anticipated time. Have you decided on the stop in New Orleans yet?" Barbara, his administrator and assistant, always had his back covered and his quick rendezvous in New Orleans was not finalized. Anything more than a few moments delay in arrival would not be welcomed by Bennett. Such was the complexity of Stephen's schedule around which changes were made with great difficulty.

"Tell Mike I will be there on time unless there are weather delays. Thanks Barbara." Stephen purposefully avoided her question on the New Orleans stop and his usual tryst there. He was hopeful he could squeeze the 'meeting' in, and Mike would just have to wait if it came to that.

A couple more phone calls and he would be out the door heading for another incredibly hectic day, and his head would not hit the pillow until late tonight. Sadly, tomorrow's schedule would be much the same.

He was not looking forward to the day and even felt a twinge of dread at facing all that he had before him. He once was driven to attain this lifestyle, and all that comes with it, but now was questioning, in his own mind, what true meaning there was to his life. He purposefully avoided that question as the answer was too painful. He just wished he could just go back to bed and hibernate.

# 6

# MEET DAVID

8:30 AM: Be careful where you stand as this kitchen is cramped so we need to be diligent. This guy is David Carpenter, 46, and a dishwasher here in the Eastside Diner just outside Ashville, North Carolina:

…

The morning breakfast rush was in full gear and the mountain of dishes and fry pans needing to be cleaned was piling up. David had been up to his elbows in scalding hot water for the last four hours scraping, cleaning and sanitizing. The work was mindless and senseless drudgery. As soon as a rack of plates was cleaned another dirty tub took its place. His gaze, when he bothered to take a look at his surroundings, was one of soap boxes, bakery racks, full and empty, antiquated huge pots and pans, a mop and rolling bucket and shelves of clean dishes, glasses and cups. Overhead were shelves of paper cups, take out boxes and bags of napkins. Regularly, one supplier after another wheeled in the back door their daily deliveries for Eastside. They often tried to get David to sign for their wares, but he always pointed with a head nod towards the front of the diner and kept about his duties. Years ago, some teenage customer left behind a transistor radio with ear plugs. After languishing in the box under the cash register for months, David rescued it and has been listening to 99 KISS, the local country radio station ever since. David was a waif of a man barely pushing 120 pounds. A five-day growth of a scraggly grey/brown beard was a constant mask on his face and when he grinned, which was very seldom, he revealed the gaps of a few missing teeth. A grungy, gray, once white t-shirt worn under a two size too big overalls was his work duds finished off by an old pair of hiking boots covered in grease and food stains. David seldom bathed and rarely did anyone notice – he was always in the back doing the dishes and seldom did anyone venture into David's domain.

Whenever he had a break in the pile of dirty plates and egg yolk crusted forks David would head out the back door for a quick butt, unfiltered Camels was his brand though sometimes he rolled his own, and he kept the pack rolled up in his sleeve. He thought that looked real cool!

"Y'all out here again? Get back in there or I'll fire you!" Reggie squawked at David.

David knew the routine, Reggie, the little mouse of a manager would always catch him hiding out with his cigs and David would have to head back to his station, but only doing so in super slow motion. "Yeah, I hear ya! You think I don't know if I can smoke or not? Get off my back you little pipsqueak" David uttered under his breath just loud enough to hear as he walked by Reggie still keeping the butt in his lips. An act of defiance that David knew would frustrate Reggie to no end, but David also knew he didn't have the authority to fire him. So, they constantly played their little game. The dishes, pots and pans got cleaned and so what if there was a little smoke in the back of the kitchen. A well-placed fan pushed the clouds of smoke out the door.

The diner was open for breakfast and lunch, so David usually worked from 6 am to 3. He usually ate a plate of greasy food around eleven, just before the lunch rush hit and after work, he usually headed down to TK's Liquor Store to buy some smokes and a pint or two of Jack Daniels. The rest of his day he would just hang out and polish off the booze before heading home to his trailer and crash. The predictability of David's routine seemed certain and hopeless.

# 7

# MEET JAMIE

8:30 AM: The last person we will observe is Jamie, three and a half, granddaughter of John and Judy Ramsey. Jamie was born in Oklahoma but moved with her family last year to Grand Rapids, Michigan. John and Judy are both teachers in the neighborhood, but their family story is not typical as you shall see:

...

There was a constant hum and beeping from the monitors in the bedroom at Blodgett Hospital. The semi-private room had a sterility and coldness about it, offering very little in comfort or amenities to visitors. Jamie's hospital bed was freshly changed an hour ago and the night nurse had been replaced by the day nurse, Amy, shortly after. The room smelled of antiseptic and bleach as Jamie's 'suite-mate' was discharged and her bed was readied for the next. The room air conditioning seemed too cool, the constant background conversations of nurses and staff, and attempted sleep in an uncomfortable chair were all added, unwelcomed irritants for Judy. She had spent the night with Jamie so John could catch up on his rest today. They took turns staying with Jamie through the night, and the strain was taking its toll on them both.

Jamie had a particularly difficult night. Judy wanted to be awake tending to her constant needs, but the stress and lack of sleep was evident in Judy, and she had just drifted off to sleep. John apparently got some well-deserved rest, and he sent a loving text to Judy, thanking her for the good night's sleep and he would get there around eleven. He would, as always, pray for her and Jamie as he drove to the hospital, but today's prayers had an increased sense of urgency. There wasn't much else that he could do but trust the Lord would take care of them and provide a healing touch. The Lord knew Jamie needed a healing and health restoration. John just trusted that it would arrive soon, very soon. "Right now, would be a great time Lord!"

It wasn't long before Jamie began stirring from her tortured sleep. Her moments of rest were few, and as the pain medicines wore off, she would wake with chilling screams of agony. Judy was ready to summon Amy with the red "Nurse" button so that Amy could react quickly with the syringe into the IV line and dispense the pain killer. If the IV timing wasn't right, it would be agonizing minutes before Jamie would tire from writhing pain. "Thank God!" Judy whispered as Jamie settled back down. It must have been a dream that roused Jamie, she thought. "Tomorrow, honey, the sun will come up tomorrow, bet your bottom dollar that tomorrow ..." Judy sang softly as she repeated Jamie's favorite song. Tomorrow they would get the results of the brain scan and fluid samples the doctors removed from the back, bottom of Jamie's skull last night. "God, please, please let it be good news tomorrow. Please." she begged and pleaded: "I don't know what I will do if ..." and she couldn't finish the thought.

Nurses and doctors came and went. All were avoiding emotion and keeping a positive attitude. Rarely was there eye contact with

Judy. It was all business and hurried optimistic gestures. The waiting for the results was having its effects on the staff as well as the family.

What was truly remarkable about this scene playing out in the hospital was that Jamie had the appearance of perfect health. Her curly golden locks rested gently on her face, ocean blue eyes were softly hidden behind her lashes, flickering as she entered REM sleep again and her breathing deepened and slowed. Judy could again relax and allow her brain to enter into that half sleep that parents somehow conjure up when needed. Half listening to Jamie and half drifting off to a desperately needed rest. "Please…" she whispered as sleep enveloped her.

# 8

# FRANK'S BACKGROUND

10:00 AM: It is now about an hour and half later. You have now met all six of our fellow brethren for the designated time. Let's look in on Frank again at his work:

...

Frank hung up with the cement guy confirming the next delivery on Wednesday. The work has been steady and paid well since he became the head construction foreman for the Hudson Building & Construction Co out of Warsaw, Indiana. The office/trailer on the site was positioned strategically so that he could view the entire housing development from his trailer window. Over the past ten years various sections of the community were added as housing lots were sold. The early morning buzz from caffeine was starting to wear off and his concentration had begun to drift. He dropped the pencil on his desk and, leaning back in his chair, stared off at the worksite, thinking back to his morning commute earlier.

For the past two weeks the radio in Frank's F150 pickup hasn't been working and the absence of background noise permitted Frank to reflect a little. His love for Darla was amazing and daily he fell deeper in love with her although this was not always the case.

"Man, she was beautiful that first day that I saw her. She wore a white blouse and a reddish checkered skirt as she walked into Mrs. Barnes' English class." Frank reminisced out loud. Frank was the wise-cracking jock sitting in the back, always quick to make note of any new cute girl in school. Darla moved to Marion in October of their junior years and although Frank thought Darla to be quite the great looker, Darla didn't even notice him. She had other interests and they were definitely not the jocks in school. She had a heart for the Lord, and she was wanting to settle into her new church to establish friends there. "There" was not where Frank was to be seen. Frank had a rebellious, smug attitude as the MVP of the Marion High basketball team that made it to the state quarterfinals in Indy last year. Hopes were high they would go even farther this year and he was the star. He was also handsome and a HUGE flirt. His greatest pleasure was to keep a half dozen girls on the line at any given moment and his wandering eye was constantly on the look out to add more. Girls fell for him like boulders rolling down a mountain but now, it seems, he had detected someone who was not falling. In fact, she was not even moving whatsoever in his direction. "Doesn't she know who I am?" he often wondered, sometimes out loud to no one in particular, as she passed him in the hallway. "Yeah, she was really something. She really presented a challenge for me." he said to himself as he pulled into a gas station.

Once fully gassed he was back on the highway again. "What was it May or early June when we first met face to face? Not sure." he questioned his memory. It didn't matter since the hormones were circulating, two people noticed each other and the meeting was inevitable. Throughout their senior year Frank and Darla were 'steady' as it was called in the day. But steady to Darla was not the same as steady to Frank. He still had an eye for other girls and only seemed to be biding his time until a better fish came along. Darla did her best to keep a lid on his flirting and rarely left him alone any time they were out. But one thing Darla had going for her was her principles and her steadfast devotion to them. That represented a challenge to Frank that reaaaalllly intrigued him. So, in a way she had her own hook in him.

They became engaged a year after high school and married a year after that. Over the next several years, they had a relatively happy marriage although Frank's flirtations and "life of the party" antics were growing rather old. Frank was a good provider, he worked hard when he felt like it, mostly to earn more money so he could party on the weekends. Darla wanted to start a family, but Frank wasn't ready, maybe he would never be ready, so he avoided the subject whenever Darla raised it. That is until Darla missed her period one month. After that, Frank had some animosity towards Darla, feeling she tricked him into becoming a father, although in truth, her pregnancy was purely accidental.

When Adam was born their relationship seemed to improve and for a year or so Frank grew into fatherhood enjoying young Adam. But soon Frank and Darla fell back into their usual ways and life just muddled along. Aimless seems to describe their once dynamic and bright future but back then it was wallowing in mediocrity.

"Man, it was tough back in those days. I really didn't have a clue." Frank polished off the last of the coffee in the thermos and climbed out of the truck. "God be with me, here goes another day!"

# 9

# SOPHIE'S BACKGROUND

10:00 AM Sophie again as she is fixing her hair:

…

"My, My! Look at the time! The whole family will be here in two hours, and I am not even close to being ready yet." Where is my brush? It was here a minute ago."

"Oh Dear, this lock of hair just won't sit right…" her thoughts trailed off to a time her mother had brushed her hair. Her mother. Mom! The earliest memories she had was working with her mother in the cotton fields singing gospel songs. It had been decades since the Emancipation, but there remained little change in lifestyle. The blacks were free but still enslaved to their illiteracy, lack of "life" opportunities, segregated cities, and discriminatory predators. It took all of the families' combined labor to cover basic necessities within their tenement shacks. If it had not been for a faith, embedded within the souls of Sophie and her family, they would have succumbed to a life without hope and a dismal future. Instead, they survived, perhaps even thrived, in spite of their circumstances. Life with faith had meaning, ensured hope and sustained the family from one season to the next.

At sixteen, Sophie first met the love of her life, Horace Campbell. He was a laborer at the Biloxi lumber mill, tall and muscular. His beautiful white teeth flashed whenever he smiled and when he smiled Sophie's heart melted. She fell in love with him when she first laid eyes on him and knew in her heart, he would eventually be her husband. The only problem was he didn't notice her for another month, until the summer church social, where they were formally introduced. Horace liked what he saw in Sophie and their love blossomed. A year later they were settling into their own little bungalow newly married, so happy in love.

Horace worked long, hard hours at the mill barely making just enough to pay the rent and put good food on the table. Their married years were the happiest of her life as she bore three boys and a girl to round out their family. Most of the time they didn't have two nickels to rub together but their love sustained them, and they raised their children in the gospel, in respect, and in love. Poor in many ways yet still very rich. Waves upon waves of sadness and grief engulfed her when Horace didn't get up for work that tragic Tuesday morning. His heart just gave out and he passed quietly in his sleep. Her world fell apart. Her husband of fifteen years … gone.

The outlook was grim for a single, middle aged black woman with four children. She scraped along by doing laundry and baking pies for the white folks across the tracks. Most meals were either beans and rice or rice and beans and on some Sundays a smidgen of bacon fat joined the menu. The rest of their diet came from the garden out back. The daily grind was backbreaking, but Sophie endured it and then some.

It was no secret how Sophie kept the children on the straight and narrow. She had the Bible for guidance and a sturdy wooden spoon for discipline. She lavished both on the children regularly. Sundays were always God's day and the whole family, dressed in their finest, proudly walked to the Mount Zion Baptist Church. They arrived early and stayed for both services 'cause Sophie thought the message might not sink in during the first'. They always, always stayed late to clean up and Sophie chatted with the other widows. Their camaraderie helped sustain Sophie.

Jesus protected her and provided for her. Make no doubt about that. There was the time when she probably would have been raped walking home from church late at night, but her attacker just hung his head and slowly walked away at the emphatic shout of the name of "Jesus". Stretching a pittance of an income to provide Christmas gifts to the four children seemed an impossibility yet every December, God provided. Sophie must have memorized half the Bible and regularly spoke the Word into her children's lives. It had a stunning effect.

# 10

## CASSIE'S BACKGROUND

7:00AM west coast. Let's see what is going on in Cassie's mind as she hangs onto life:

...

Through the fog of pain killers Cassie was in a happy world reliving a time in her youth. It was the late seventies, and she led the youth-group music-ministry at the huge "Christ's Followers Church" in Houston. All the kids loved her, and she loved them back. Cassie took the time to get to know each and every child that crossed her path. She had the "gift" of service and used it well. "The kids" as she called them, were hungry for the Word and she enthralled them with stories current for the day but embedded with truths from the Gospel. Every Sunday the Kids went home with a new biblical principle to entwine in their lives.

That personal touch she poured into her ministry soon caught the attention of the senior staff at CFC and they moved her up in responsibilities to coordinator of the Overseas Ministry. Her management skills grew the ministry three-fold in two-years, allowing CFC to stretch the gospel to thirty-three nations all starving to hear the Truth. Cassie even spent a two-month stretch in Bolivia to further hone her credentials.

It wasn't long before she was promoted to the position of Manager of the Houston Homeless Center. Working with James Ludington, the local real estate magnate, Cassie established a series of homeless shelters that more than met the area's needs. Before long, she became the center's Director, accomplished while finishing up on her master's degree at SMU. After graduation, she became Assistant Minister at CFC and a few years later Head Minister. Her personae and leadership skills were magnetic and soon she was involved in local politics. Cassie gained fame running the campaign for the governor in the '98 elections. She was a woman whose career was soaring yet her entire life was a facade.

# 11

# STEPHEN'S BACKGROUND

10:00AM: Back to Stephen heading for the airport:

…

The back seat of the limo was quiet, only interrupted by the sounds of occasional splashing when the limo ran through puddles. Stephen's brain was tired from the preparations back at the office, so he took a few moments to close his eyes and just relax.

His mind drifted off to Sarah, his wife of ten years who had just divorced him and he was fine with that. Her constant harping on him about family and church had not worked and would never work. He just couldn't understand how someone could be so weak in her thinking. God having a personal relationship with "me"? How foolish to believe in such things! Good to be rid of her and her Jesus too.

His cellphone broke his train of thought, Barbara explained there would have to be a change in the flight plan he filed the day before. Seems there was some issues with weather popping up over the Carolinas and he would have to revise the plan before takeoff.

Stephen made a mental note to re-file the plan with the changes, then settled back into his thoughts. Life always seemed to be gilded for Stevie, as his grandfather always called him. Stephen hated that nickname and always refused to acknowledge it. At four, when other kids were playing with their dolls or tricycles Stephen was learning basic economics and practicing lacrosse with his trainer. Junior high brought the first of a constant line of girls, then women into his life. He was easily bored with cooings of "love" and "going steady". He was interested in being a pilot, same as his uncle, and they regularly went up for a ride. In high school he founded the flying club and while soloing at ten thousand feet, discovered the only real peace he would ever know.

Stephen's Grandpa and Father made their millions in the railroads. Millions is an understatement in that there never seemed to be an end to the money supply that Steve needed while growing up. Always a new car, more extravagant vacations, or clothes. It would be so easy to fall into a "rich kid" lifestyle and just live fat and happy off the "old man's" money. But Stephen had a drive that he would make it bigger than either Grandpa or Dad. His yardstick would be money. All that remained was to see how long it would take.

He easily became the Valedictorian of his preppy east coast high school, the boring one that all the "Richies" sent their spoiled brats to. Number one in his graduating class at Columbia in Environmental Science. Number one in his post-graduate class at Harvard. His doctoral thesis "Climate Change Effects in the Modern Sub-Sahara" was cherished reading for all the high brows in the environmental/activist circles. He later confided to an associate that he made up most of the data just to tweak the snobs. He gained notoriety far and wide with his opinions on global warming then global cooling just to be controversial. Whatever his stance, that became "settled science". What really surprised him was how easily deceived the general populace was on the Climate Change issue. It was entirely fabricated just to create a controversy from which to siphon off money from the wealthy through offsets and taxes, while lining the pockets of the liberal experts. It was way too easy, almost like printing money.

His success in business and consulting garnered even more accolades. His presence on the roster at conferences ensured a sell-out. His public relations manager was quick to have Stephen in front of the cameras as he spoke out for one charity after another, although rarely did any charity receive any of his money. It was usually more of a token donation since Stephen felt the masses were the right ones to support such causes and, after all, he did give them his endorsement. What more did they really need? He was constantly on the go, flying his private jet from conferences to pricey consultation sessions, to testimonies before congressional committees, and to high end charity dinners. Stephen was in high demand and high demand was his selling price, always covered by the legions of super-rich, like-minded, far-left Liberals. It was all a game and Stephen played it better than any. His "yardstick" surpassed his predecessors years ago. He was the 'winner' or so he thought.

# 12

## DAVID'S BACKGROUND

10:00AM: Careful of the slippery floor, here's David:

...

The morning routine was dragging on as David was working his way through the pile of dirty dishes. If it wasn't for the mindless aspect of the job allowing David to escape into his thoughts or music, then he would have checked out of this job years ago. The radio was broadcasting 99 KISS in his earplugs, but his brain was elsewhere daydreaming about nothing in particular. KISS was playing a sentimental love song about a mother and her little boy when David's brain caught the phrase "Mommy, I love you." Like an avalanche, his emotions welled up inside him, "Mommy!" he thought. His earliest memories were, as a two-year-old, rocking in his mother's arms after awakening from one of his many nightmares. His mind was conflicted between the horror of his dreams and the adoration of his mom. This scenario must have repeated itself dozens of times over David's first five years: always his mother was falling, twirling and tumbling away from him and then the next moment she was drying his tears and consoling his deep sobbing. Bizarre was the perfect word to describe his emotions even though he never heard of the word.

It seemed as though these dreams suddenly stopped when he turned five, about the same time his mom started talking to him about her new-found faith in Jesus. David's anxiety about his mom abandoning him, just like his dad did when he left three years ago, was relieved by a father figure in Jesus. Up until that time it was just David and Mom. Now it was David and Mom and Jesus – his new heavenly father.

David would fantasize how he would go fishing with Jesus, talk with Jesus, hug Jesus and best of all be hugged by Jesus' strong and protective arms totally enveloping his small frame. He would hold that moment in his mind for as long as he could before the world penetrated his peace. David was complete and never felt 'being loved' so deeply. Then it all ended.

Mom left David in an auto accident as a drunk plowed into the driver's side of their car. That was the last time he saw his mom. Then there was only David and Jesus. David became angry when Mom was gone and implored Jesus as to why! Silence was all he heard from Jesus who had abandoned him as well. Then David was alone and broken.

He was always alone as he moved from aunts to cousins to grandmas to foster homes. He was incredibly alone. He was drifting through life, always searching and never finding, always hoping yet always disappointed. Always.

David's schooling was consistently mediocre. Not that he lacked talent nor intelligence. He just didn't have any motivation. He got out of life what he put into it which was not much.

He graduated high school and was eager to be out on his own. He moved into a rather spartan apartment, though he rarely spent any time there. He drifted from meaningless job to meaningless job living paycheck to paycheck. Slowly spiraling downward, slowly losing a desire to strive.

David tried to keep an outwardly happy mask on his inwardly sad emotions. He attracted women who had a penchant for fixing men. After they had tried to work their wiles in "straightening out David" they soon grew frustrated, abandoned him again, like his mother, and his loneliness returned even when another lady took over. The cycle repeated itself over and over.

Such was life for David. Year was followed by year, decade by decade. The man in the mirror staring back at him was growing gray and haggard. His life was sameness and aimless. The ladies stopped trying to fix him and the jobs seemed to be filled by younger and younger applicants, not that he really cared anymore. He was stuck plain and simple. He was stuck at five years old and as hard as he tried and as much as he wished he couldn't get past being five.

The clanging of pots brought David back to reality. The cook liked to toss pans at David, sometimes landing in the sink and splashing. He knew this irritated David a lot but David endured the bully secretly plotting ways to get revenge. Once the dishes were done then David dove into the pans. He was making quick work of the tasks before him when, it hit him like a charging rhino, the chest pain, an ache in his jaw and a tingling left arm. He fell to one knee, grabbing his chest, and struggled to pull in a breath. His teeth were clenched tight in pain, and he staggered trying to retain his balance. He was losing consciousness, the kitchen was a blur, and he fell face first onto the grimy, greasy floor. Someone called 911.

# 13

# JAMIE'S BACKGROUND

10:00 AM: Let's catch up on Jamie:

...

Judy awoke to a monitor beeping annoyingly; Jamie's heartrate was slowing which triggered an alarm. This happened occasionally over the past couple of days and Judy learned it was nothing to be concerned with. Judy was awake now and after getting herself some coffee she settled in again next to Jamie. They had been through so much during the three and a half years Jamie had been with them.

Like many children born into a drug abusing family, Jamie's story is quite typical. Mom did pain pills while dad snorted cocaine and smoked weed all day. Jamie would normally flounder in such a home, but the paternal grandparents would not let that happen. John and Judy were at the hospital when Jamie made her appearance in this world and they quickly, with the help of Child Protective Services, obtained custody and brought Jamie home.

For the next three plus years John and Judy poured their love into little Jamie. She thrived in their care, under their protection, bathed in their love. She became the darling of the social circles she inhabited, charming all with her endearing smile and sparkling personality. In her nursery school she quickly captured hearts and her personae commanded the room. In Sunday school she would absorb the Bible Stories and replay them over and over with Gamma and Papa at bedtime and she even took to memorizing verses each week.

One particular aspect of young Jamie's life was how she was having a profound effect on her mom and dad. During their weekly visitations over the past couple years, they were slowly turning their lives around. Not only were they giving up their drug induced lifestyles but were making great progress in their parenting classes. Soon they would be having over-nights with hope of integrating Jamie into their lives full time. Perhaps most amazing was how Mom and Dad had started going to church recently. They were not only growing closer to Jamie, but they were also growing closer to God and each other. Jamie's love of life was drawing in all those around her. Ten days ago, life took a difficult right turn.

# 14

# FRANK'S ENCOUNTER

11:30AM: You may have noticed that I have not been very engaged with the individuals up to this point. There is a reason for this, I am strictly prohibited from outwardly influencing them – I can only suggest or make impressions in their mind. I have a small voice that I try to use to motivate and inspire. You might compare me to the little angel on the proverbial shoulder, but I am far from that. Observe Frank again:

...

The roofing crew finished house #42 and headed over to #43 when they discovered the shingles for #43 were not the specified color. Frank was quickly summoned on the wireless and was brought up to speed. "Can't anything go right?" he protested. He soon found out the distributor had also discovered the error and had sent another truck with the correct color roofing a half-hour ago. Since it hadn't arrived, the supplier sent out a search car to find the truck. Frank slammed the phone down. "Get the roofing crew over to #46 and help them finish off that one" Frank barked to his head roofer.

Over the next hour Frank checked in at each job site to see how they were doing. The odds of finishing on-time were appearing more and more remote, and this ate at his stomach. He chewed a handful of Rolaids and trudged back to the trailer. "Lord how are we gonna get this done?" he offered as a prayer.

Frank reflected back to another previous time where God got him out of an impossible situation. It was about seven years ago just after Adam was born. He and Darla were having a rough stretch financially, and to escape Frank spent a couple of nights a week at the Mucky Duck Saloon down on Meridian St. There he ran into an old flame from high school. Now, one thing you must remember about Marion is it's a small town and everybody knows everyone, so news of an affair, particularly involving an ex-star athlete, spread like wildfire. The news found its way to Darla the next morning and emotions were boiling over by dinnertime.

He swore he would change and be a better husband and father. She threatened divorce, and just wanted out. He begged and pleaded for forgiveness. Darla was skeptical. His track record was poor at best, but she finally relented for the sake of Adam.

"You will do this MY way or else its over!" she demanded. He was in no position to argue and agreed to all her terms. First there will be no more evenings out of the home. When he is not working, he will be with her unless she can verify where he is. Second, Frank will have to start attending church with the family, no more sleeping in on Sunday. And finally, she will be managing the finances of the home, at least until things are turned around.

Pretty stiff rules Frank had to admit. But he could handle it. He really loved Darla deep inside and couldn't imagine being without her. So, there he was sitting in the First Methodist Church on Charles Street the next Sunday.

...

Here is where I enter the picture. You see Frank just cannot handle Darla's demands on his own. He needs to be changed from the inside out and cleansed of his lusts and cheating spirit. I whispered into the mind of Pastor Thomas that Frank is in need of salvation and must have a word from the Pastor to make this happen. Now, Pastor Thomas is usually not too responsive to my suggestions, but somehow on this day he leaned in a little more than usual and heard my voice.

. . .

"Mr. Benjamin, how did you like the service?" the Pastor offered as Frank was heading for the door.

"Oh fine." replied Frank with his eyes still up ahead.

"Can I see you for a moment?" The question just hung there for all nine months of a pregnant pause.

. . .

Frank, you have to listen to the man. He just might be able to point you in the right direction. Remember your promise to Darla! You are going to need a lot of help to stay on the straight and narrow. Just see what he has to say, and then ask him if he could give you some advice, you know, now and then.

. . .

Frank felt a stirring in his soul. "You know Pastor, I would like to talk to you for a little bit."

"Fine! Come over here where we can speak in private. Don't worry, Darla will wait for you." the pastor reassured.

"Yeah, I suppose so." acknowledged Frank. He was open to all that the Pastor had to say that day about turning his life around. Frank got saved and learned that he was now a different man. The old Frank was gone, and the new Frank and loving husband and father remained. The Pastor's words were etched in Frank's heart, and it allowed him to see Darla in a totally different light. His love for Darla overfilled his chest and it poured out through his eyes like a blubbering little baby. Frank didn't care. His life was turned upside down. Nothing else mattered. He was in love. Really in love for the first time in his life, and when he smiled at Darla, she knew it too.

That miracle not only turned around his home life, but his work life as well. Old "Frank" would work hard all week to make as much money as he could so he could party all weekend. The new "Frank" put in extra time cleaning up the work site, and he even started mentoring a few of the younger guys on how to work more efficiently, taking time to be sure the job is done right the first time. He taught the guys how to be invested in their job, and career and that it can pay off in the long run. He even started caring for some of them in a personal way, sort of like a big brother. They all cherished the new Frank and so did Frank's boss – so much so that he promoted Frank to head foreman. Life had been good and was getting better ever since.

# 15

# SOPHIE'S LEGACY

11:30 AM: Sophie, back in the dining hall, all gussied up like a flower, or rather a daisy:

...

The guests for lunch started arriving a half hour ago, and the size of the family was overwhelming for Daisy. Sure, she at one time could name the names and recite their lineage, and how they were just a joy to be around. Now everyone seemed to be all grown up. Their little faces were still familiar, but they all seemed to be so much older. Never the mind. Sophie was having the time of her life. Grinning and twinkling. Look over there, all her kids were getting set to take a picture. Her kids! Her Kids...

Robert, the oldest became a surgeon at the Biloxi Hospital. He worked his way through school washing dishes and pumping gas at the all-night filling station. When he left home for college Sophie was so proud, she couldn't stop crying, for you see Robert was the first ever in his extended family to make that trip to college. Everyone in town was pulling for Robert to succeed and he did. He really did, eventually becoming a world class heart surgeon at

Johns Hopkins. When he retired, Robert had seventeen children and grandchildren who all went through college.

Jeremiah, second oldest, was a lawyer and ranked first in his class in law school. His path to scholastic excellence was funded through his minor league baseball career. Although he never made it to the big leagues, Jeremiah was a fanatic about saving his money and went to school part-time throughout his career. Joining the prestigious law firm of Holmes and Bryan in his early thirties, Jeremiah quickly rose to Associate and finally full partner. He is still working today doing mostly pro bono work for those who never had quite the same shot in life that he was given.

Carla, the only girl, was a whiz in school rising to class Valedictorian when she graduated a year early. Education was her passion and she passed through her college years in a blur. She couldn't wait to graduate so she could sit at the front of the class at her old elementary school. She was a natural for the job and motivated virtually every one of her students to excel in their studies. She even attended the graduation ceremony of the students from her first class and, wouldn't you know it, every one of them presented her a rose. This show of love for her was repeated at every graduation for the next thirty years, so many roses!

Baby Roger, he is always Sophie's baby, was the quiet and insightful one. He would forever bring home any and all sorts of frogs, cats, bugs and critters to care for. "But they're homeless" he would implore as Sophie marched him out the back door to turn loose most of the animals. Roger always befriended that one little boy who needed a friend and, more times than Sophie could remember, came home with a fat lip from standing up for some neighborhood kid who was being bullied. In school Roger was a daydreamer and just barely managed to graduate after Sophie had a talk with Mr. Davis, the High School principal. Seems the guy needed to get some common sense "straight talking" from Sophie as to why it was so important that Roger be graduated. You see, Roger was accepted into the ministry at Mount Zion Baptist becoming the assistant to the head minister and needed that diploma. Roger found his calling and, after he finished the studies, headed back home to his Mount Zion Baptist family where he was destined to become head pastor.

Sophie was proud of her family and regularly thanked God for all her blessings. The family had all arrived and she slowly sipped her lemonade on the sofa in the dining hall of her nursing home. Her legacy secured, her work complete.

# 16

## CASSIE'S DOWNFALL

8:30 west coast time: It's getting quiet now in the Daniel's home, let's observe Rhonda who has so faithfully attended to Cassie's needs:

...

Rhonda looked upon the frail skeleton that once was her lover. "Oh, what could have been!" Rhonda whispered knowing Cassie was too comatose to react. She sat stoically at the foot of Cassie's bed as the storm began to pour again. The lights flickered and thunder rumbled across the valley. The morose weather only deepened the depressing atmosphere in the home.

Three years had passed, almost to the day since Cassie's career blew up. Being a senior aide to Texas' U.S. Senator James Cromwell she had to manage the media, appointments, back home constituents and the onslaught of lobbyists. Those lobbyists were the worst, constantly demanding favor in each and every bill, as if their dollars really bought them that much influence. Cassie had to pay lip service to their belligerent needs. She had a loyal staff that fulfilled all these duties and it was Cassie who they really propped up. Her drinking was having its effect on the grassroots workers. Cassie became arrogant and overbearing in her daily demands and impossible deadlines. It was impossible to please her, and rarely did she smile but even then, only through getting revenge against those who crossed her. Cassie's bitter life was careening out of control and some of her shady deals with the oil barons were unraveling.

"Those sneaky reporters are digging where they shouldn't and I'm going to see that they are stopped!" She confided with her staff. Her tirade raised many an eyebrow and the seeds of Cassie's demise were beginning to ensnarl her office like a boa squeezing its prey.

Senator Cromwell broke the news first. In actuality he was told to break the news so that his office would not be dragged through the mud of the scandal. The Attorney General was beside Cromwell placing the blame squarely on Cassie. As she was watching this on the news, she could hear the commotion of the FBI making their way through the office intent on placing Cassie under arrest. The perpetrator walk into jail was absolutely humiliating and the hand-cuffs chaffed at her wrists.

Staffers spilled their guts in exchange for immunity, influence peddling charges were fabricated then filed, and blustery speeches were made by political hacks who were also worried their own scandals would be revealed. The whole affair was swept under the rug when Cassie took the fall. The charges were later dropped but the damage had been done. Cassie was the scapegoat and life inside Washington went on. "Cassie who?" people would be saying in another six months as her scandal would soon be forgotten.

Her relationship with Rhonda was stretched thin and her finances were in ruins. As if that were not enough, Cassie's health took a turn with all the stress. After visits to several doctors, a diagnosis was given, and it was grim: pancreatic cancer was detected in several lymph nodes. She was given one to three years with no hope for remission. The diagnosis was a shock and seemed to be the uppercut that took all the steam out of Cassie. She never regained her stamina or stature and her life had been a long and slow downward spiral ever since.

Rhonda often reflected on the course their lives had traveled. There were so many turn offs on their road that they could have taken to have a happier and fulfilled life. Now all that remained were regrets.

# 17

# STEPHEN'S SCHEDULE

11:30: Back to Stephen at 24,000 ft. – somewhere over Georgia:

...

The flight from LaGuardia to Tampa was uneventful. The ground traffic was backed up a half hour and his flight plan was revised to fly around the thunderheads over Charlotte. Taxiing for take-off was maddeningly slow and his patience was growing thin as he finally got to the end of the runway. Forward throttle and he would soon leave his cares behind him. The sensation of pure power that explodes from the jet engines never failed to excite Stephen and his pulse raced as the throttles were pushed forward and he was pushed back into the comfortable leather chair. He hit the minimum speed for takeoff halfway down the runway and as the wheels lifted off he soared off upward at a nearly forty-five degree angle. Moments later he was above the clouds. Bliss. After getting past the air traffic around DC-Philly, Stephen turned the autopilot on and relaxed for the short hour before he would start his descent into the Tampa-Orlando airspace. The landing was typical, and the limo met him as he got out of the jet.

His agenda for the day: A quick flight in his Learjet 45XR and he would be in Tampa by noon where he would address the annual conference of Gulf States Environmental Health Association. Next a quick stop in New Orleans to meet Sandra if he could get out of Tampa on time. Then on to Dallas to make an appearance at the Hemmingway Journalists League, his "favorite" media association. Favorite because of his exaggerated fee they always pay. Finally, off to Chicago and a dinner with the local political cronies. The topic of his keynote address is "How to use the environmental cause to extract maximum benefits for local politics". The Chicago stop definitely conflicted with his overall environmental integrity positions but Steve was assured his comments would not leave the room, besides they paid very well. A tiring flight home and a cool half million would be deposited into his bank account.

# 18

# DAVID'S ROOMATE

11:30 AM: We are now in the Intensive Care Ward at Parkside Hospital. David arrived about an hour ago:

...

David recalled a moment when someone was pounding on his chest as lights and yelling surrounded him in a foggy haze. The next coherent thought he could remember was one of a dreamy beeping in his ears. His blurry mind wondered if he was in heaven but the muffled voices in the next room dispelled that thought. He was still alive, and the world was spinning as the painkillers were doing their job. He slowly turned his head and spotted a monitor with green 'blippy' lines slowly marching from left to right. A steady "beep, beep, beep" beat out like a metronome that coincided with the thumping in his chest. David, for some reason had survived a massive, deadly heart attack.

In the other bed of his intensive care suite lay another survivor although what his journey was remained unclear. "Johnny" was the only name that David caught as they gasped out their names in introduction, handshakes not attempted for the obvious obstacles of too many tubes, IVs and monitors. Johnny had a magnetic personality and a crazy sense of humor. Just the person that David needed to lift him up at this time since David was having remorse and regrets as to why God had spared him.

"David, what happened to you?" Simple question. David wondered if he should even answer such a loaded question.

"Not sure what you mean Johnny. You know I had a heart attack." He deflected.

"No, I guess I wasn't clear. I meant; how did you end up here stuck in a bed next to me? What is your life's story that would lead you to this point in your life?" From there David told of his life from his earliest recollections up until his collapse into the greasy floor of the Eastside Diner. Johnny interrupted on occasion to ask for clarification to understand David's life. "Wow!" Johnny added at the conclusion of David's story. "You have had a rough life."

Johnny offered in return, "Me? Well, my story isn't a whole lot different." and he went on for the next hour vividly describing one story after another interlaced with such humor that it made David's sides hurt from all the laughter. It was a great reprieve for David since these moments were rare in his life. They both traded jokes and generally enjoyed each other, David felt like he was finding a friend, forming a bond, and fulfilling a void that had existed for so long in his life.

...

The moment has come, Johnny. This man next to you has suffered greatly from his early years and he desperately needs to be introduced to his savior. Don't wait for you may not have another chance. If you do not act now, he will never have another opportunity.

...

Johnny could sense that David needed some direct talk and assessed his situation. "David?"

"Yeah, heh heh, what is it?"

"I feel compelled to ask you a serious question so I would like a straight answer without interjecting any humor. You have told me of your experiences with Jesus as a small child. Would you like to meet that Jesus again? Would you like to feel his arms around you and rest in his love?"

David's eyes began to well up with tears. While choking back his emotions he blurted out "Johnny, you have no idea how much I would love that."

"Well, it's very easy. Just repeat after me. Lord I am a sinner and I come to you for forgiveness of my sins." David repeated. "I repent of those sins. You are my Lord and Savior, and I will worship you all my days." David repeated. "That's it. You are now saved; your sins are forgiven and you are a new man. Now be bold, be vulnerable and dare to ask Jesus to wrap his strong arms around you again."

David closed his eyes and almost immediately his face grew into the widest smile and then into a soulful expression of such gratitude that he couldn't contain his tears. David sobbed and sobbed and sobbed.

# 19

# JAMIE'S DIAGNOSIS

11:30 AM: Back in the hospital room with Jamie:

...

Jamie woke from her sleep, the first stretch of solid sleep in a couple of days. Remarkably the pain medication was still working, and Jamie was in a playful mood, a rare opportunity for Judy to spend a few quality moments with Jamie. After a quick bowl of Fruit Loops, the two of them were snuggling down for a command performance of *Curious George Goes to the Hospital* her most favorite story in the "whole-wide world." She could relate all too well to George going to the hospital and when George gets better at the end of the book, well, that is how she wants her story to end too.

As Judy was reading the story, her thoughts drifted back to early last week when her whole world changed. Jamie had spent the afternoon playing at her best friend's house. They had a heated swimming pool and hot tub that Jamie liked to play in. Judy regularly went with Jamie to offer additional supervision and the afternoon of play was uneventful and would easily have been chalked up to a fun and unremarkable August day.

Five days ago, Jamie had a very hard day. She came down with a fever, nausea, a bad headache, and vomiting and it came over her very quickly. In the morning she was fine, and by afternoon her health took a nosedive.

Her symptoms were so severe that Judy and John rushed her to the ER to see just to be cautious. The doctors and staff were efficient and compassionate. Blood tests were ordered, all negative. A thorough physical was performed, again nothing of concern.

The doctors were pretty much stumped, and they admitted Jamie into the hospital for additional tests. Over the next couple of days Jamie's symptoms were mitigated by pain meds and she remained calm but rather drowsy. Test after test came back negative and the situation had the doctors completely baffled. Two days ago, while Jamie was somewhat coherent, she told Mommy her neck was bothering her, "sort of stiff and achy" as she described it. Judy comforted Jamie and reassured her it would be OK. Later in the afternoon Judy happened to mention Jamie's neck comments to the attending nurse. One of the attending physicians overheard Judy and his face went pale. Bacterial Meningitis was his obvious diagnosis, and he sprang into action. Antibiotics were ordered to begin immediately, and the usual spinal tap was scheduled for later that evening. Hope was restored, after a few days in the hospital and ample time on the meds Jamie should be home within a week. Everyone slept well that evening as the verifying test was performed and sent off to the lab.

Yesterday the confirming test results were given to the doctors, and they were astonished that their diagnosis was not confirmed. Meanwhile Jamie was not responding to the antibiotics. Her situation was getting worse. Exasperated parents, patient and hospital staff were at a loss as to why Jamie was not getting better. Last evening the head neurosurgeon suggested to Judy and John the problem may be PAM.

"PAM? Pam who?" Judy demanded.

"Not PAM a person," reassured the physician, "PAM" is a disease similar to the Bacterial Meningitis we once were concerned about, but I am afraid this one is not very promising. Jamie probably will not survive if the confirming tests are positive. You see, PAM is caused by a one cell organism, an amoeba, that might have infected Jamie's brain but in this part of the United States the disease is very rare. The amoeba thrives in warm fresh water, usually in the ponds and lakes in the southern states. Cases like this are very rare in Michigan with the colder temperatures.

"Mrs. Ramsey, is it possible that Jamie was on a trip to Texas or some other southern state in the past week or two?"

"No, she has been here in town the whole summer. Since she hasn't been down south, is it possible you are wrong in the diagnosis? Couldn't it be something else?" Fear was overtaking Judy's voice and tears were welling in her eyes. Panic was washing over her in waves, and she started to tremble. John's head was swimming and his knees began to buckle and he steadied himself against the bed.

"It may well be something else. I certainly hope so. Remember we are just guessing at this time but we need to rule this PAM in or out so I have scheduled the procedure, a quick test to draw fluid from Jamie's brain. After that, well, we will just have to see. The results will take about 24 hours."

The doctor's reassurances were not helpful. Judy sensed deep in her soul that it probably was PAM. The symptoms lined up too exactly with what was going on with Jamie. But Jamie hadn't traveled down south, so how could... Judy stopped in mid thought, and she felt a punch to the gut that doubled her over in absolute pain.

"Of course, the hot tub at the Bakers' house. Jamie was in their hot tub! John, oh John! Call the Bakers! They have to be warned." The rest of last night was a whirl of phone calls, samples from the hot tub rushed to the lab, and then hurried waiting. Anxiety and wishing the results would be negative, but silently preparing for an inevitable positive. Time stood still. Breathing became difficult. Everyone was fearful and were praying with a vengeance.

# IT IS APPOINTED

# 20

# THE OBSERVER'S PLEA

We have observed a great deal about each of our brethren: Who they are, what their background is, what motivates each, how their lives have turned out so far, and more.

As we visit each one again you probably will find it very difficult to remain silent and not do something to interfere with fate. I can certainly understand your feelings and desire to help.

You must resist those temptations and trust that I know what I am doing. Remember our title verse – "And as it is appointed unto men once to die, but after this the judgment." from the book of Hebrews. Each and every person has an appointed time to die. That time is set by God, and it is his decision to impose the end of each person's life to align with his greater plan. In time you may know why God has called someone home, perhaps you will never know. God can see far into the future, and he can foresee reasons that things need to be the way they are. You only need to trust God and rest assured in the knowledge that He loves you more than you can ever know.

Please keep these thoughts in mind as we observe each person one more time.

# 21

# FRANK'S DEMISE

1:11 PM: Back to Frank, who is feeling the pressure of finishing the job:

...

It was getting late, and Frank really needed those shingles on the site now! His wireless squawked that the truck was pulling in front of #43. Frank barked in the wireless that the original crew from #43 should head over and help unload the shingles. Work needed to start immediately.

Frank grabbed his hard hat off the rack and headed out the door. On the way to #43 he made a quick stop at two of the other sites and offered encouragement to those crews and even chatted with one of the guys that was having a little trouble with alcohol. After talking with Frank, he seemed encouraged and hurried back to his task.

Once at #43, Frank began directing traffic and workers to hasten the unloading. It was taking way too long to get things going and Frank was strained at his limit for patience. After another handful of Rolaids, Frank decided he would direct the lift operator to locate the pallet of shingles up to the peak of the roof.

It is somewhat ironic that time, which once seemed forever while waiting for the shingles to arrive now has slowed to an absolute crawl. Frank's attention was diverted momentarily by his wireless ringing, his mind, while consumed by five or six other pressing issues, was diverted to the handset and he grabbed his two-way to answer with urgency. The lowering of Frank's hand to answer the wireless seemed to be a signal to the lift operator that he should drop the load. The pallet load of shingles shifted when the load was placed on the angled surface of the roof. Before the operator could react the bundles of shingles spilled off and to the right. There were several other workers watching the load shift and fall. They all instinctively jumped to assist. Shouts of warning were formulated in brains and were about to erupt as the bundles began to fall. Frank got his hand on the wireless and was just pushing the talk button when a blow to his head and shoulders forced him forward and down. The lift operator jumped from his seat and was half-way to the ground when the load landed, his cry of warning just emerging from his lips. The other workers were half-way standing when Frank crumbled under the weight. The otherwise tranquil morning of typical labor sounds was engulfed in shrieks of warning and terror. Frank crumpled under the massive weight and force of the heavy load, bones were broken, his flesh was torn, his body buried. Then there was silence. The sort of silence where disbelief is deposed by reality, where momentary hope is defeated by a cruel gravity, where thoughts of "Frank! Move!" twisted into "God! Oh no!"

In the chaos that ensued the guys leapt to the pile of shingles with Frank at the bottom, people were yelling, and bundles and shingles were pulled from the pile, shouts of "CALL 911" and "Get that bundle off Frank's back" were yelled at no one in particular. Finally, they got to Frank.

He was in terrible shape, dazed and morbidly hurt. Slowly, with great pain and effort, Frank mouthed the words "Tell Darla I love her." He coughed, and his body writhed with pain. Every muscle went limp. Just like that, Frank was gone.

SOPHIE's last twinkle

# 22

# SOPHIE'S REST

1:11 PM: Sophie, having just finished her lunch had planted herself on the couch in the main dining room:

...

"I am sooo happy with all my family here. I'll just rest a bit and catch my wind." She explained as she dropped into her usual place on the community sofa just inside the Dining Room. The joy of festivities had thrilled Sophie so much that she seemed to have a hard time catching her breath. Sophie was taking this all-in stride for she knew her time was not far off. Being over one hundred taught her to recognize how she was feeling and what was going on within her body. She could tell she would not be here long. It wasn't that she was sick or failing in her mind. It's just that her body was worn out and tired. It had been through enough.

The family mood was respectful and cheerful. Lots of laughs, some tears, some prayers as many realized they might never be all together again! Roger led the crowd in a prayer for Sophie and went on for about twenty minutes, recalling humorous episodes of spanking spoons, memorizing verses, and skipping school; serious moments of gratitude and honor for the matriarch of the Campbell family. He just wanted to honor his mother on this fine occasion, as the "Circle of Life" was poised to gather another ring with the upcoming wedding.

All the happiness of the family pleased her so, and to see so many of them together at one time gladdened her heart. Roger's prayer and recollected stories entertained her, and she had a few of her own that she could add. But she remained silent and just listened, smiled and twinkled. Sophie became quiet as the emotions laid bare by the festivities swirling in her mind. Exhaustion seemed to blanket her frail body. It seemed she was drifting off to a different kind of sleep, an eternal sleep when she caught herself, like the moment just before you fall asleep, and the body relaxes. She smiled purposefully closed her eyes and with that she fell silent and slowly entered into eternity.

# 23

# CASSIE'S CHOICE

10:11 AM west coast time: Here again with Rhonda and Cassie:

...

Cassie's mind was usually numbed by the constant morphine shots that Rhonda had been administering. Cassie was seldom lucid enough to offer any conversation but on this particular day Cassie was as moody as the weather.

...

Rhonda, please try one more time to speak to Cassie. Her time is very short, and she needs to hear of the hope of salvation, just like she did back in the youth group. Please hurry and don't be timid.

...

Rhonda felt a strong need to console Cassie offering hopeful words to sustain her in the remaining hours. Rhonda even tried to draw memories from Cassie about her earlier ministries when she was a woman of purpose, and leadership, and faith.

Cassie would have none of it. "Why do you torment me with the past? I cannot change it!" Cassie chewed into Rhonda. "The past is better off left dead as I shall soon be. I have nothing more to say."

And with that Cassie collapsed into a deep, deep level of unconsciousness. Rhonda began to tear up and for a moment felt so sorry for Cassie. Rhonda kept thinking "We could have been so different. If only you could have changed. What a waste. What a waste"

Cassie's breathing slowed and became very shallow. Her eyelids flickered as if they were trying to wake up. Her lips parted and her hand went limp. A final exhale escaped from Cassie's lungs.

Rhonda, overcome with inconsolable grief, sobbed a gut-wrenching long wail from the bottom of her heart.

# 24

# STEPHEN'S FINAL FLIGHT

1:11 PM: Back to Stephen in the cockpit leaving Tampa:

...

The pre-flight checklist seemed to drag on forever, little quirks that usually are forgotten seemed to get under Stephen's skin. The part of his agenda that was tightest from a time perspective was the flight to Dallas and the little delays were becoming big annoyances. Stephen seemed intent on making the stop in New Orleans and the delays were making it more and more difficult. He could be able to make up the delays once in the air, but Stephen wanted to get going now and not have to deal with the stress.

The storms that were making their way across Tampa Bay were building and heading towards the airport. The southern winds dictated that Stephen would have to take off over the bay and his opportunity to take off was slowly evaporating. Finally, his turn to take off was ready. He radioed the tower "49er110 ready for take-off." The tower answered back an unintelligible reply garbled by the crack of a lightning bolt breaking from the thundercloud. Stephen interpreted the answer as permission to take off and shoved the throttle forward. The tower screamed back at Stephen to turn back but Stephen was intent on leaving and would have no part of another delay. He didn't care. His only mission was to get to the end of the runway. He flipped off the radio.

The jet literally leapt off the tarmac and bolted down the runway. Faster and faster the jet engines screamed as it careened down the wet runway, now becoming slick from the pelting rain. Just a few more knots and the jet lifted off the runway and was blown to the left as it started to gain altitude. The Lear jet climbed as quickly as possible, and Stephen veered it to the right trying to avoid the immediate wall of menacing clouds but it was not enough. As quickly as he entered the cloud a down draft threw the jet into a downward pitch and a roll to the left. The sudden change in direction snapped the tail rudder in half and he headed straight for the bay. Stephen didn't have time to radio Mayday before he slammed into the shallow waters at 300 knots. One second Stephen was yanking on the controls, trying to pull out of the spin, the next second splash, mud, impact, and a micro-second of pain. Then quiet.

# 25

# DAVID'S LAST EMBRACE



*1:11 PM Back in the Intensive Care Ward at Parkside Hospital:*

…

David was intoxicated with the love he was feeling. Johnny just watched in amazement at the joy that had overcome a man who was so broken. The depth of feeling exhibited by David was such that Johnny had never seen nor imagined. David was like a five-year-old again and was able to move forward, to start his life anew. David's demeanor reflected he was a changed man. All this emotion had an exhausting effect on David, and he became very quiet, contemplating his new-found freedom. Joy danced in his mind as he drifted off to sleep truly happy for the first time in decades.

As the final tears collected on a saturated pillow, David's body went limp, the monitor stopped its beeps and changed to a constant "eeeeee", the blips on the screen turned into straight lines. Emergency staff responded as they were trained to do, but Johnny knew their efforts wouldn't bring David back.

Johnny whispered to himself, "It's almost as if Jesus kept David on this earth just long enough to wrap his arms around him one last time. See you soon, my friend, see you soon."

# 26

# JAMIE'S PRAYER

1:11PM: This is truly a sad situation at the hospital with Jamie. Her case is always one of the toughest for my brethren and their families:

...

Jamie's vitals started heading south an hour ago. John was summoned to the room as were Jamie's mom and dad. There was a somber mood in the room. Judy and John could only hold Jamie's hand and silently cry. Their beautiful granddaughter was in her last hours and grief was painted on their faces. There were waves of anger, and shouts of frustration and pain at the reality of what was happening. Everyone in the room would have gladly traded places with little Jamie. Doctors and nurses were crying in the hall. Strangers who passed by the room when told what was going on would lapse into tears as well. Jamie had touched so many in her short life. She had taught everyone who encountered her life that there is beauty in believing.

John and Judy' pastor, Greg Harper, arrived and assessed the situation, Jamie's condition, and the mood of the mourners. He asked everyone to bow their heads.

…

Greg, you need to be bold at this moment. I will help you select the words you need to say. Please trust me, lean in and speak from your heart.

…

He paused for a moment to assess his thoughts "Lord, I ask that you comfort those in this room and beyond. Be gentle and soothe the hearts that are broken. We grieve for our Jamie whom we love so dearly, carry us in our need. We grieve, not as the world grieves, but we grieve with hope, and the knowledge and the truth that there is a God, and his name is Jesus. He came to this world so that we might have abundant life, an eternal life through Him, and that eternity is for all to share who believe in Him. This life is but a vapor, and we are all appointed to pass through the veil of death. Some of us when we are in our nineties, and, tragically, some of us in our youth. Those of us destined for eternal life have no worry. We can face death without fear because our faith is in the one who died for our sins, who has made us, who sustains us, and who calls us home when our work on this earth is over. But that is not, thank God, that is not the end, but only the beginning. We have heaven waiting for us and a reunion with our loved ones. Therein lies our hope. Lord, if it is your will, we beg that you will restore our Jamie to her full and complete health, and if you call her home, Lord please usher Jamie into your heaven, into your arms, and into your love. Amen"

Tears again started to flow, the family formed a group hug, the room grew silent, and Jamie slipped through the veil, through the veil to her eternal healing, through the veil to eternal happiness and joy, and through the veil to her eternal, adoring, heavenly Father.

# 27

# THE SIX BRETHREN

Frank stood there watching as the EMTs worked feverishly over his body. The faces of his co-workers were twisted, masks of shock, disbelief, and grief. Most of these tough construction workers had tears in their eyes. Frank turned around to survey the scene which was gradually starting to fog over as if a mist was appearing between him and the death scene. At the same time as he was turning, he was confronted with an opening. Not really a door but an entry way that beckoned him inward. Most peculiar of all, he knew intuitively he must enter and so he did.

Sophie, still in a bit of a trance, stood up without her walker, on the other side of the room, and watched as her family started to realize she had passed away. The impact of her death was hard on her immediate family, but they all were standing with their arms raised, and joy on their face even though tears were streaming down their cheeks. Sophie tried to speak but no one heard her. She started to turn, noticed the family was starting to fade away, and a portal or opening appeared in the dining room wall behind her. Her instinct was to enter it which she did without any fear or hesitation.

Stephen was amazed he had survived the crash. He was standing on the water looking down at the remnants of the aircraft. Fuel was covering the water around him, and it was on fire. Strange that he did not feel the heat! Then it dawned on him he must be dead. As he contemplated this predicament, the watery grave below him started to disappear. Looking up he discovered an opening into which he raised himself up, and in. Why he did this, he didn't know, only that he knew he must get into the opening.

Cassie looked down upon her emaciated body. On the far side of the bed Rhonda was deep in her grief. Cassie felt giddy being rid of that body with its pain, agony, loneliness and depression. While at once happy she was also filled with fear as to what would happen next. With that thought the room started swirling in a dense fog. A quick turn to her left and she faced a brightly lit hallway into which she felt compelled to enter.

David stood in the entrance of the room where the STAT team was working feverishly. He knew he didn't wish to be back in his old body, but he was fearful as to where he would be headed next. As he was watching the hurried activity before him, the room started to grow fuzzy and gray. David wasn't sure what was happening, but he noticed a set of doors that he felt he should enter. There was peace about him as he went inside.

Jamie saw her parents and grandparents crying but she was not sure why. There were a lot of people in the room all with sad looks that she couldn't understand. Jamie wanted to cheer the people up and make them happy, but the room started to swirl around her and she was getting a little dizzy. Then she noticed this beautiful staircase rising from the room. Jamie knew she needed to see what was at the top and started climbing the steps.

In the next moment, the six were standing in a plain, nondescript, perhaps even generic, room. Everyone was quiet.

# AFTER THIS

# 28

# THE OBSERVER REVEALED

Hello, please do not be afraid. As each of you entered the doorway, mere moments ago, you all entered directly into this room with me and my guest observer. You came here from your earthly towns of Marion, Biloxi, New York City by way of Tampa, Sacramento, Ashville and Grand Rapids. Here, as you might not guess, is nowhere but, I will assure you, soon you will arrive at your eternal home.

We have observed a great degree about each of you over the last several hours. We've become aware of your life situations, the choices, both good and bad, you have made, and saw the manner and circumstances of your death. Each of you passed away around the same time.

The Bible says, "And as it is appointed unto men once to die, but after this the judgment." Each of you have died and now comes the reason why you are here. This judgment will fulfil God's promise described in the book of Hebrews for those of you who are familiar with that verse. For those of you who are not, well, you will still be judged. Ignorance is not an excuse because each of you has had multiple opportunities to choose to believe in God or choose to not to believe, and each have made your own choice. At this point, you cannot change your mind. Your fate is sealed.

I am the Holy Spirit, a full partner with God and Jesus and together we comprise the Godhead three in one – Father, Son and, yours truly, Holy Ghost. Each of you have heard my voice whispering in your mind's ear over your lifetime. Some believe me to be a conscience though they are misinformed. I have been pointing each of you to Jesus Christ ever since you were born. I have been prompting you to worship, give to the poor, help the sick, and feed the hungry. It has been my voice that has been comforting you when you were fearful, when you were grieving, when you were lonely, when you were sick. I pointed you to Jesus, the one who takes away your fears, who heals you, who mends the broken heart and chases disease away. I consistently and continually pointed you to Jesus, the one who died for your sins, the one who can forgive your sins and who can cleanse your soul. You may not have heard my voice, but you did feel a sense that you needed to do something, and either followed that sense or ignored it. What you did with my promptings was your choice and yours alone.

The Bible says the wages of sin is death. That is true for you, who are standing here, as it is true for every person on the earth. The Bible also states that all of mankind, each and every one, is sinful and must pay the consequence which is death. No one can escape this final fate.

The process from here forward depends on how you lived your life, and the choices, or most importantly, one choice you have made. You will remain here with me until your name is called. At that time, you will enter through that door ahead of you and undergo your judgment. Is there anything you would like to ask me?

Yes – Frank?

…

"Can I get a message to my family?"

…

No. However, depending on how your judgment goes, you may see them again and soon. The concept of time passing can seem very different there. Anyone else?

…

"Are you also with my family at the same time as you are here?"

…

Good question Sophie. Yes, I am present with your family, I am there with all your families right now, for those who by faith accept me and the love I desire to give. I am omnipresent, meaning I am everywhere. That concept seems difficult for most to grasp. Let's just says I exist beyond the limitations of time and location.

…

"Can you speak to Ronda and entice her to change her life?"

…

I constantly advocate for people to make the right decisions in each of their lives. When they are open to a change, they may feel my urgings a little stronger and interpret my voice with more clarity. When they are set in their ways, it is very difficult to feel my promptings.

God has given everyone free will. Rhonda has had freedom to live her life as she wishes, whether it is in line with my promptings or not. That free will can serve to do well or serve to do evil. Without free will, God could force you do good, worship him, and so on, even if you do not feel that in your heart. What God is looking for are those who willingly submit, with humility, to His better plan. Does anyone else have a question? Very well, please relax and take a seat. You'll be called momentarily.

# 29

# STEPHEN WRIGHT!

"Stephen Boyd Wright" came a voice that emanated and re-sounded from everywhere. It was calm, yet so authoritative, that one could not even consider disobeying or hesitating.

Stephen slowly rose to his feet and glanced at the faces of the remaining five people in the room. Their expressions were blank, as if they were not even aware he was called. An all-encompassing fear gripped Steve as he inched toward the door. It opened inward to a dark room. When he was a few steps inside, the door closed behind him, and he stood in complete darkness and absolute silence.

In what seemed like hours he began to notice, more as an impression than as a vision, a video or movie of sorts starting to play out in front of him. This was not your typical movie, but it was in three dimensions, and he was a participant. It was his life in rewind as he witnessed every instance, he broke one of God's commandments. With each sin there was an opportunity to avoid that sin, but he chose to commit the sin instead. What should have taken weeks to review such a voluminous presentation only took, what felt like, a couple of minutes. After that, he saw person after person who had tried to speak to him about Jesus and His love. The desire of his wife's heart was for him to consider Jesus. His friends, people at work, at college, in high school made attempts to get through to Stephen; even his two grandmas. Throughout all that he was watching, Stephen could clearly see that he was indeed a sinner, although he really didn't think he was all that bad. He could also see there were too-many-to-count opportunities for him to choose Jesus over his lifetime, and on every occasion rejected the offer. The evidence was damning, there was no trial, no defense that he could offer. The proof against him was his life. He was incredibly guilty, and he knew it. All that was left was the verdict, the sentence, the judgment and he knew it was coming.

Once Stephen came to the realization of his guilt, the room brightened to near sunlight, emanating from Jesus, sitting on a throne so immaculate and glorious that its beauty cannot be described. Surrounding Jesus were countless angels tending to every thought and expression. The sheer majesty and magnitude of splendor, mercy and grace overwhelmed Stephen. The mere sight of Jesus, the most holy, caused Stephens knees to give out and he fell flat on the floor, face down. Stephen closed his eyes as tight as he could, but the light still penetrated.

**"Stephen, what do you have to say regarding your life?"**

Stephen could only mumble something totally incoherent. His intention was to say, 'totally guilty of all my sins and I throw myself at your mercy'.

Jesus, of course, knew that.

**"You have sinned the same as everybody, but you still carry those sins before me. I cannot let you go further. As much as I had loved you over your lifetime you continually rejected me. Each time my heart broke and tears filled my eyes. Yet even though you rejected me, I still would have**

received you if you had changed your mind right up to the instant of your death. Since you did not, I can only pass judgment on your soul based on your choices. That judgment is for you to enter into the place of eternal damnation and torment. So be it from this moment until the end of eternity! "

Stephen disappeared and in his next breath inhaled a burning smell of sulfur. Thus began his eternal separation from God's love engulfed in agony and alone in anguish.

# 30

# CASSANDRA DANIELS!

"Cassandra Daniels" was called next although the remaining four were unaware she was getting out of her seat and heading towards the door. This should be a piece of cake she remembered thinking as she entered through the door.

Once past the threshold, Cassandra was standing in total darkness. For what seemed like hours she finally started to see pictures or something about her life from a young girl. Each scene she saw how she had sinned and its effect on those who were close to her. A lifetime of sins that were embarrassing and condemning. There were no excuses for her sins because she knew right from wrong and purposefully caused each and every one of them to occur. In every instance there was a way out that she could have taken if she desired, but her choice of the sin was more compelling and satisfying to her fleshly desires. All the sins were exposed, right up to the time of her death. After that she saw those instances where she had the opportunities to choose Jesus and there were times and occasions where she did choose Jesus, but her motives were insincere.

Cassandra always chose to make herself look good in all her works serving the Lord. Her conversion was from a former sinful life to a new sinful life of self-importance, self-service and ego building. The Holy Spirit could not penetrate such sin and was not welcomed in Cassie's life.

Cassandra immediately understood that her life as a Christian was a façade. She was in it for fame, fortune and the praise of others. The 'show' of Christianity was on many occasions a stumbling block to many who looked to her for spiritual leadership, but they were scorned by her egotistic desires. Some never again returned to a point of accepting Jesus solely because of what Cassandra did. Horror and shame washed over her as the consequences of her actions and decisions became evident.

Upon this realization, the brilliance and glory of the throne of Jesus appeared before her. The mere impression of being in the presence of Jesus caused her to throw herself onto the floor. The fear and full significance of her failure, in a Christian life, was all too clear. The breadth and scope of her sins was apparent to her, and she was in agony.

**"Cassandra, what do you have to say for your life? "**

Cassie could only weep and gnash her teeth. She had studied the Bible and she was now fully aware of the consequences of her life choices.

**"I can tell you are ashamed and aware of your decisions over your lifetime. Cassandra, I loved you from the moment you were born, and I set in place a destiny of greatness before you by serving me with your life. Early on you professed to love me, but you were merely serving for your own ego. Countless times the Holy Spirit pleaded with you to change**

your direction and follow my path for your life. Countless times you chose yourself. My heart ached every time you rejected me, hoping you would change, fearful that you would not. Right up to the time of your death you could have change your mind, repented and asked me into your heart. You knew the consequences, but you refused. You rejected me time and time again. As a result, you know that I must reject you. Your cold and callous ways condemn you to the place of torment and anguish. I wish it were not so but that was your choice, and this is my judgment."

The next moment Cassie was alone, forever separated from God's love, forever inflicted with searing pain, relentless anguish and hopeless despair, regret and loneliness.

# 31

# FRANK BENJAMIN!
# SOPHIIE CAMPBELL!
# DAVID CARPENTER!
# JAMIE RAMSEY!

All four rose simultaneously, each unaware the other three were also rising and walking toward the door. All four entered an open door and stood silently in the darkness.

Not one of the four were forced to look at their history of sins and lost opportunities to turn to Jesus. There is one simple reason: not that they had lived perfect lives, but their sins were forgiven and forgotten. Each had taken the opportunity to receive God's gift of salvation and receive God's gift through the re-birth of their spirit. They had surrendered and repented and turned from their wicked ways. There were no sins to condemn, their sins were washed away by the blood of Jesus. There would be no trial because there was no evidence of any wrongdoing, there would not be a conviction for no guilt was found. There would, however, be a judgment and it was 'NOT GUILTY'.

The darkness evaporated and standing before them was Jesus. The glory and holiness overwhelmed all four and they reverently recognized their King and knelt before their savior offering praise and worship from their lips. Jesus came to them, gave each their crown of salvation and wrapped his arms around each of the four welcoming them to the entrance of Heaven:

First, He spoke to David – **"I am so proud of your love for my embrace. You experienced my love as a very young child. Every time you imagined that I was holding you, hugging you, caring for you – I truly was. I was there as the Holy Spirit comforting you. Then when you lost your mother, you rejected me. For far too long I ached to hold you again and you evaded me.**

**It took laying on your death bed for you to finally allow yourself to accept me again though the witness of your hospital roommate, Johnny. How I rushed to you in your need and I hugged you with the love that you missed for decades. I loved you as only I can. I am so, so glad you accepted my love again. That is why you are here. You repented of your sins and turned to me, you were broken, and you turned to me for healing, your pride and suffering were too much for you to endure into death and you finally came home. Welcome home!"**

Next, He turned to Frank. **"Frank, you were a very stubborn man. You had your life going your way – good looks, basketball, fame, and the attention of all those girls. You were in danger of getting into the sins of the world so deeply that**

I couldn't ever reach you again. That is why I sent Darla into your life. She had my love shining out of her soul and that attracted you. It took you a long time to confront the decision to reach out to me and accept my free gift, my gift of salvation, my gift of the rebirth of your spirit. You buried the old man ad became a follower. You humbled yourself and noticed my love shining from your wife. At that moment you were truly married to her, and you began to realize what love really means. You put aside the spiritual rags of your former self and accepted my riches. Welcome home!"

He smiled and embraced Sophie: "**Oh Sophie, my beautiful child. How long I have waited to see you face to face. Your long life testified to your devotion to your husband, your family and to me. From the time you were a baby your life was infused with the good news of the gospel. Your life was one of poverty and great difficulty and I was with you every step of the way to protect you and offer provision. Your family is your legacy. I know how proud you are of them because I am so proud of them too. You were truly handed a life of lemons and you served lemonade to others all along the way. Your smile and my twinkle in your eye served as a testament to your life of sacrifice, serving, giving and loving. You never had to choose to accept my gift of salvation, be-cause you embraced it from infancy, and you lived your life accordingly. After more than a century it gives me the great-est of pleasures to say to you – Welcome home!"**

Finally, He bent down on his knees to speak to Jamie: "**My precious child. You have touched my heart every day of your**

**life. Born into a difficult family situation and raised by your loving grandparents, your life truly blossomed in the midst of a broken family. I am so greatly pleased that Gamma and Papa came along to bless you in your life. They poured my teachings and love into you, and it was all good. Your short life was packed with testimonies of your love for me in song, verse and play. Your natural beauty was magnified by your faith.**

**Although you have missed your chance to become an adult, you will have the greatest of opportunities to mature in heaven. Past members of your family will be there to enjoy your new life with you; and it will not seem long before Mom and Dad, as well as Gamma and Papa, will all come to join you here. I am so happy to have you here with me. Welcome to heaven!"** As Jesus stood, he picked up Jamie with his strong and mighty arms and placed her gently on his shoulders. She giggled with delight.

The walls of the room around them dissolved away and they were standing in the midst of the glory of Heaven – it was indescribably perfect, far beyond any imagination.

# Epilogue: The Observer

I'm afraid you will have to leave now. You cannot enter with these four because your time has not yet come. You will have to put down your book and go back to your life as I continue on with my work.

But remember, I am never far from you, and I will leave you with this: You will remember what you have seen and heard when you were with me and because of this you are now accountable for knowingly either embracing or rejecting God's magnificent gift of love.

While the deaths of the six brethren in this story may seem tragic or, maybe in a way, justified depending on the character, I hope you will take away this reality: it does not matter what your sins, how bad or how well your life was lived, no matter what your life circumstances may be. There is one, and only one, way to get to heaven and that is through your acceptance of God's gift of salvation, your repentance of sins, and your acceptance of Jesus as Lord and Savior. God will see your heart and will know if you are sincere or merely trying to avoid a punitive final judgment.

Also realize that, like some of the characters in the book, one's final day and final hour remain unknown. It would be easy to surmise that some would be very shocked when they woke up on August 23rd and discovered their final day was at hand. Some were prepared. Some not.

Today might be your day and if you have not made that decision to accept the 'gift' from Jesus then you could be standing before Him wishing you did. Will you be ready to face your own judgment?

You did very well on the tour, and it was a pleasure to have you with me. If you are so inclined, please pass this novel along to someone you love. Goodbye for now and I promise to stay in touch.

# About The Author

The author of "After This" is Randall Johnson. Randall began his writing career after retiring from a corporate career of over 35 years. His earlier career was filled with full-time work, raising three sons and a daughter, and performing the constant maintenance on a 1940's cape style home. His early life was spent growing up in Michigan and rooting for the Spartans at MSU while getting a bachelor's degree in Package Engineering. GO GREEN!

Randall and his wife Cynthia met in 1984 while both worked at Eastman Kodak Co., were married two years later and settled in Fairport, New York. They have been active in their church throughout their marriage and also enjoy traveling, boating, biking and dining out.

If you would be so kind, please leave your comments about this book at r.s.johnson.author@gmail.com